Amelia Bedelia

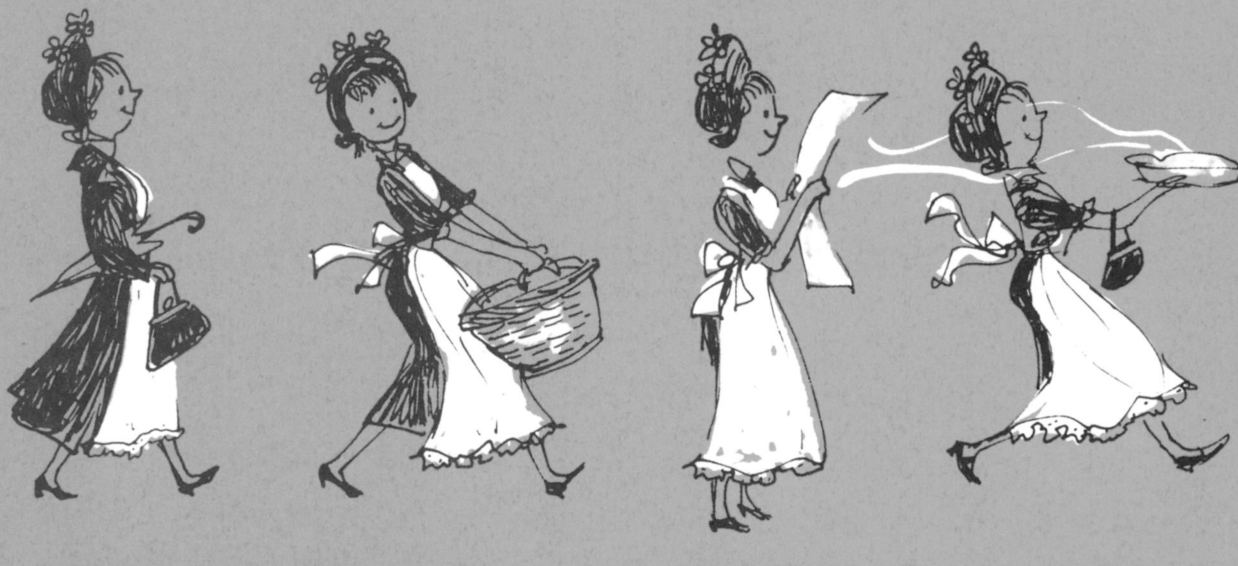

Amelia Bedelia

by Peggy Parish
Pictures by Fritz Siebel

GREENWILLOW BOOKS
An Imprint of HarperCollinsPublishers

AMELIA BEDELIA

Text copyright © 1963 by Margaret Parish; renewed 1991 by Peppermint Partners, LLC.
Pictures copyright © 1963 by Fritz Siebel; renewed 1992 by the Estate of Fritz Siebel
Additional material specific to this edition copyright © 2013 by HarperCollins Publishers;
copyright © 2013 by Peppermint Partners, LLC.; and copyright © 2013 by the Estate of Fritz Siebel

Amelia Bedelia is a registered trademark of Peppermint Partners, LLC.
All rights reserved. No part of this book may be used or reproduced in any manner whatsoever
without written permission except in the case of brief quotations embodied in critical articles and reviews.
Manufactured in China.
For information address HarperCollins Children's Books, a division of HarperCollins Publishers,
195 Broadway, New York, NY 10007.

ISBN 978-0-06-220969-6 (trade bdg.)
Library of Congress Control Number: 2012944351

Original hardcover edition published in 1963 by Harper & Row; anniversary edition
with additional back matter published in 2013 by Greenwillow Books
The Library of Congress catalog card number for the earlier edition was: 63-14367

15 16 SCP 10 9 8 7 6 5
Greenwillow Books

For Debbie, John Grier, Walter, and Michael Dinkins

"Oh, Amelia Bedelia, your first day of work.
And I can't be here. But I made a list for you.
You do just what the list says," said Mrs. Rogers.
Mrs. Rogers got into the car with Mr. Rogers.
They drove away.
"My, what nice folks.
I'm going to like working here," said Amelia Bedelia.

Amelia Bedelia went inside.

"Such a grand house.

These must be rich folks.

But I must get to work.

Here I stand just looking.

And me with a whole list of things to do."

Amelia Bedelia stood there a minute longer.

"I think I'll make a surprise for them.

I'll make a lemon-meringue pie.

I do make good pies."

So Amelia Bedelia went into the kitchen.
She put a little of this and a pinch of that into a bowl.
She mixed and she rolled.
Soon her pie was ready to go into the oven.
"There," said Amelia Bedelia. "That's done.

Now let's see what this list says."
Amelia Bedelia read,

Change the towels in the green bathroom.

Amelia Bedelia found the green bathroom.
"Those towels are very nice.
Why change them?" she thought.
Then Amelia Bedelia remembered
what Mrs. Rogers had said.
She must do just what the list told her.
"Well, all right," said Amelia Bedelia.

Amelia Bedelia got some scissors.
She snipped a little here and a little there.
And she changed those towels.

"There," said Amelia Bedelia.
She looked at her list again.

Dust the furniture.

"Did you ever hear tell of such a silly thing.
At my house we undust the furniture.
But to each his own way."
Amelia Bedelia took one last look at the bathroom.
She saw a big box with the words *Dusting Powder* on it.
"Well, look at that.
A special powder to dust with!"
exclaimed Amelia Bedelia.

So Amelia Bedelia dusted the furniture.
"That should be dusty enough.
My, how nice it smells."

Draw the drapes when the sun comes in.

read Amelia Bedelia.
She looked up.
The sun was coming in.
Amelia Bedelia looked at the list again.
"Draw the drapes?
That's what it says.
I'm not much of a hand at drawing, but I'll try."

So Amelia Bedelia sat right down and she drew those drapes.

Amelia Bedelia marked off about the drapes.
"Now what?"

Put the lights out when you
finish in the living room.

Amelia Bedelia thought about this a minute.
She switched off the lights.
Then she carefully unscrewed each bulb.

And Amelia Bedelia put the lights out.
"So those things need to be aired out, too.
Just like pillows and babies.
Oh, I do have a lot to learn.

"My pie!" exclaimed Amelia Bedelia.
She hurried to the kitchen.
"Just right," she said.
She took the pie out of the oven
and put it on the table to cool.
Then she looked at the list.

Measure two cups of rice.

"That's next," said Amelia Bedelia.
Amelia Bedelia found two cups.
She filled them with rice.
And Amelia Bedelia measured that rice.

Amelia Bedelia laughed.
"These folks do want me to do funny things."
Then she poured the rice back into the container.

The meat market will deliver
a steak and a chicken.

Please trim the fat before you
put the steak in the icebox.

And please dress the chicken.

When the meat arrived,
Amelia Bedelia opened the bag.
She looked at the steak for a long time.
"Yes," she said. "That will do nicely."

Amelia Bedelia got some lace and bits of ribbon.
And Amelia Bedelia trimmed that fat before
she put the steak in the icebox.

"Now I must dress the chicken.
I wonder if she wants a he chicken or a she chicken?"
said Amelia Bedelia.
Amelia Bedelia went right to work.
Soon the chicken was finished.

Amelia Bedelia heard the door open.
"The folks are back," she said.
She rushed out to meet them.

"Amelia Bedelia, why are all the light bulbs outside?"
asked Mr. Rogers.
"The list just said to put the lights out,"
said Amelia Bedelia.
"It didn't say to bring them back in.
Oh, I do hope they didn't get aired too long."

"Amelia Bedelia, the sun will fade the furniture.
I asked you to draw the drapes," said Mrs. Rogers.
"I did! I did! See," said Amelia Bedelia.
She held up her picture.

Then Mrs. Rogers saw the furniture.

"The furniture!" she cried.

"Did I dust it well enough?" asked Amelia Bedelia.

"That's such nice dusting powder."

Mr. Rogers went to wash his hands.

"I say," he called. "These are very unusual towels."

Mrs. Rogers dashed into the bathroom.

"Oh, my best towels," she said.

"Didn't I change them enough?" asked Amelia Bedelia.

Mrs. Rogers went to the kitchen.
"I'll cook the dinner.
Where is the rice I asked you to measure?"

"I put it back in the container.
But I remember—it measured four and a half inches,"
said Amelia Bedelia.

"Was the meat delivered?" asked Mrs. Rogers.
"Yes," said Amelia Bedelia.
"I trimmed the fat just like you said.
It does look nice."
Mrs. Rogers rushed to the icebox.
She opened it.
"Lace! Ribbons!
Oh, dear!" said Mrs. Rogers.

"The chicken—you dressed the chicken?"
asked Mrs. Rogers.
"Yes, and I found the nicest box to put him in,"
said Amelia Bedelia.
"Box!" exclaimed Mrs. Rogers.

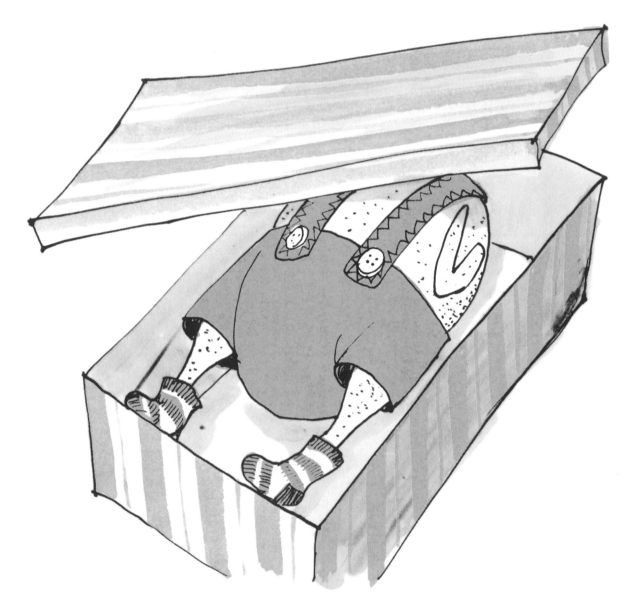

Mrs. Rogers hurried over to the box.
She lifted the lid.
There lay the chicken.
And he was just as dressed as he could be.

Mrs. Rogers was angry.

She was very angry.

She opened her mouth.

Mrs. Rogers meant to tell Amelia Bedelia she was fired.

But before she could get the words out,

Mr. Rogers put something in her mouth.

It was so good Mrs. Rogers forgot about being angry.
"Lemon-meringue pie!" she exclaimed.
"I made it to surprise you," said Amelia Bedelia happily.
So right then and there Mr. and Mrs. Rogers decided
that Amelia Bedelia must stay.
And so she did.
Mrs. Rogers learned to say undust the furniture,
unlight the lights, close the drapes, and things like that.
Mr. Rogers didn't care if Amelia Bedelia trimmed all
of his steaks with lace.
All he cared about was having her there to make
lemon-meringue pie.

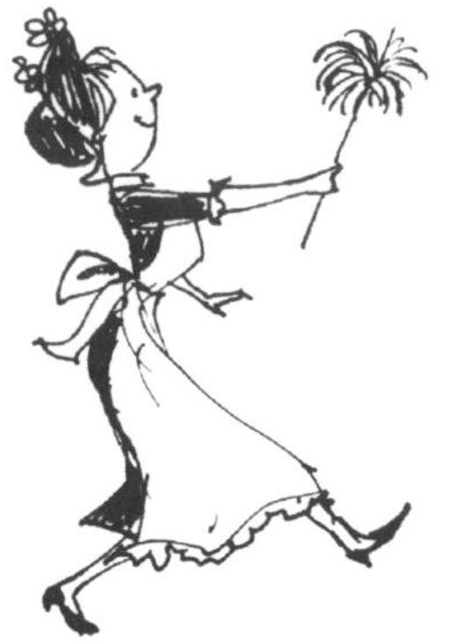

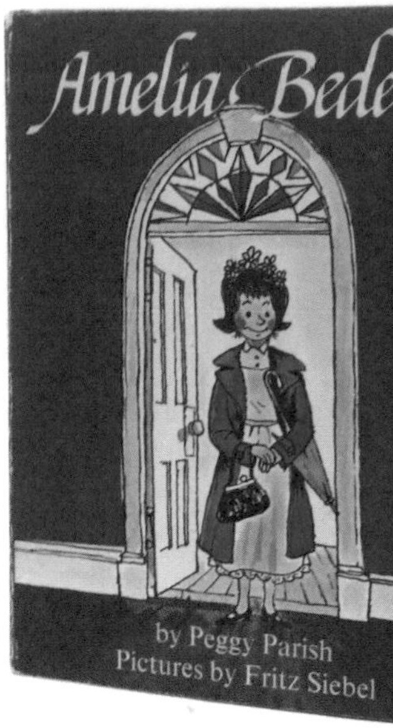

"Amelia's faux pas are indeed noteworthy. This conscientious cleaning lady arrives at a new home for her first day of work and sets about performing the chores on her list. The way she interprets putting out the lights, drawing the drapes or dressing the chicken is likely to revolutionize housekeeping in many families! Artist Fritz Siebel has given her an enchantingly zany countenance."
—*The New York Times*, November 10, 1963

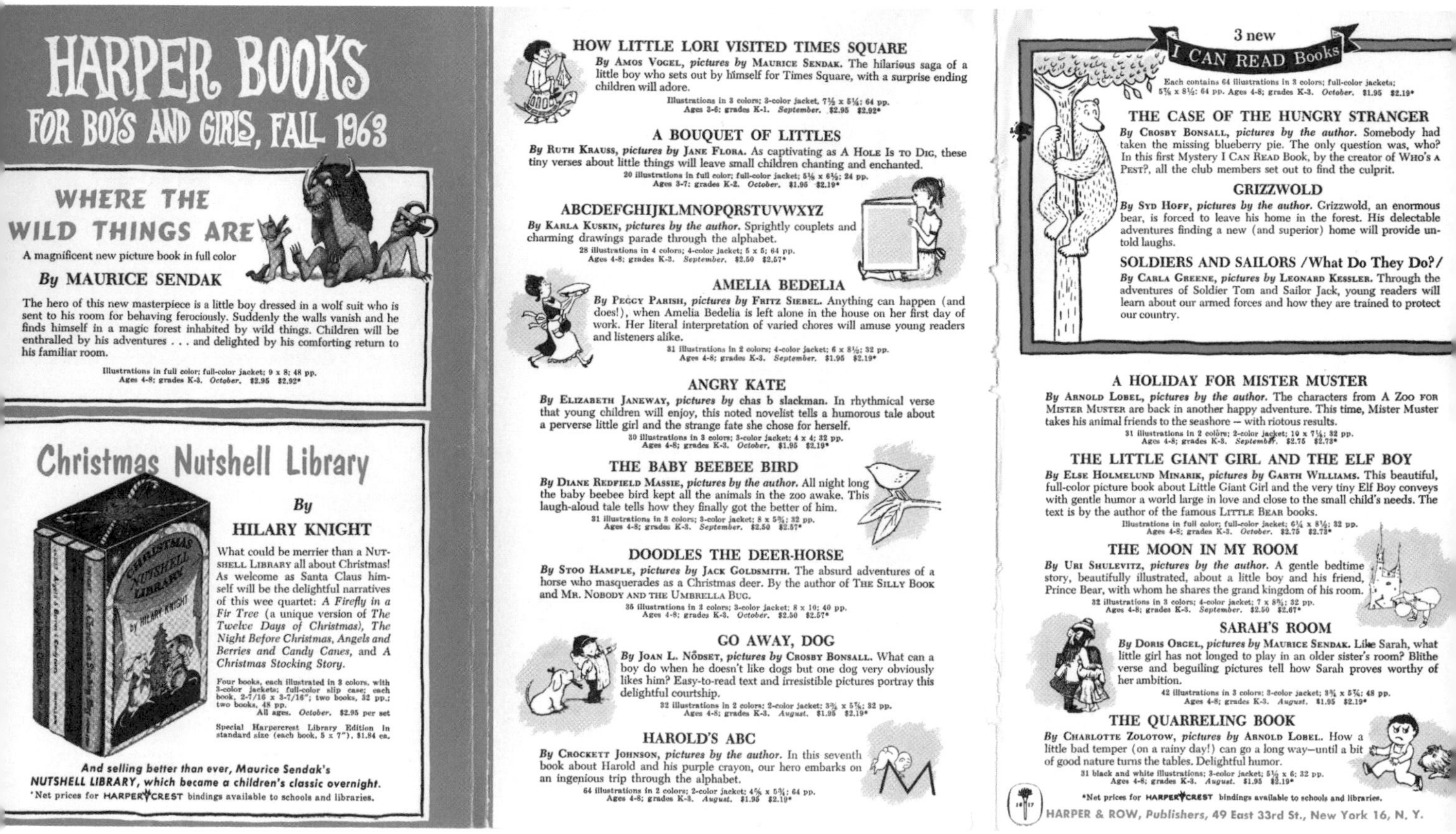

HARPER BOOKS
FOR BOYS AND GIRLS, FALL 1963

WHERE THE WILD THINGS ARE
A magnificent new picture book in full color
By MAURICE SENDAK
The hero of this new masterpiece is a little boy dressed in a wolf suit who is sent to his room for behaving ferociously. Suddenly the walls vanish and he finds himself in a magic forest inhabited by wild things. Children will be enthralled by his adventures . . . and delighted by his comforting return to his familiar room.
Illustrations in full color; full-color jacket; 9 x 8; 48 pp.
Ages 4-8; grades K-3. *October.* $2.95 $2.92*

Christmas Nutshell Library
By HILARY KNIGHT
What could be merrier than a NUTSHELL LIBRARY all about Christmas! As welcome as Santa Claus himself will be the delightful narratives of this wee quartet: *A Firefly in a Fir Tree* (a unique version of *The Twelve Days of Christmas*), *The Night Before Christmas, Angels and Berries and Candy Canes*, and *A Christmas Stocking Story.*
Four books, each illustrated in 3 colors, with 3-color jackets; full-color slip case; each book, 2-7/16 x 3-7/16"; two books, 32 pp.; two books, 48 pp.
All ages. *October.* $2.95 per set
Special Harpercrest Library Edition in standard size (each book, 5 x 7"), $1.84 ea.
And selling better than ever, Maurice Sendak's NUTSHELL LIBRARY, which became a children's classic overnight.
*Net prices for HARPERCREST bindings available to schools and libraries.

HOW LITTLE LORI VISITED TIMES SQUARE
By AMOS VOGEL, *pictures by* MAURICE SENDAK. The hilarious saga of a little boy who sets out by himself for Times Square, with a surprise ending children will adore.
Illustrations in 3 colors; 3-color jacket, 7½ x 5¼; 64 pp.
Ages 3-6; grades K-1. *September.* $2.95 $2.92*

A BOUQUET OF LITTLES
By RUTH KRAUSS, *pictures by* JANE FLORA. As captivating as A HOLE IS TO DIG, these tiny verses about little things will leave small children chanting and enchanted.
20 illustrations in full color; full-color jacket; 5⅛ x 6½; 24 pp.
Ages 3-7; grades K-2. *October.* $1.95 $2.19*

ABCDEFGHIJKLMNOPQRSTUVWXYZ
By KARLA KUSKIN, *pictures by the author.* Sprightly couplets and charming drawings parade through the alphabet.
28 illustrations in 4 colors; 4-color jacket; 5 x 5; 64 pp.
Ages 4-8; grades K-3. *September.* $2.50 $2.57*

AMELIA BEDELIA
By PEGGY PARISH, *pictures by* FRITZ SIEBEL. Anything can happen (and does!), when Amelia Bedelia is left alone in the house on her first day of work. Her literal interpretation of varied chores will amuse young readers and listeners alike.
31 illustrations in 2 colors; 4-color jacket; 6 x 8½; 32 pp.
Ages 4-8; grades K-3. *September.* $1.95 $2.19*

ANGRY KATE
By ELIZABETH JANEWAY, *pictures by* chas b slackman. In rhythmical verse that young children will enjoy, this noted novelist tells a humorous tale about a perverse little girl and the strange fate she chose for herself.
30 illustrations in 3 colors; 3-color jacket; 4 x 4; 32 pp.
Ages 4-8; grades K-3. *October.* $1.95 $2.19*

THE BABY BEEBEE BIRD
By DIANE REDFIELD MASSIE, *pictures by the author.* All night long the baby beebee bird kept all the animals in the zoo awake. This laugh-aloud tale tells how they finally got the better of him.
31 illustrations in 3 colors; 3-color jacket; 8 x 5¾; 32 pp.
Ages 4-8; grades K-3. *September.* $2.50 $2.57*

DOODLES THE DEER-HORSE
By STOO HAMPLE, *pictures by* JACK GOLDSMITH. The absurd adventures of a horse who masquerades as a Christmas deer. By the author of THE SILLY BOOK and MR. NOBODY AND THE UMBRELLA BUG.
35 illustrations in 3 colors; 3-color jacket; 8 x 10; 40 pp.
Ages 4-8; grades K-3. *October.* $2.50 $2.57*

GO AWAY, DOG
By JOAN L. NÖDSET, *pictures by* CROSBY BONSALL. What can a boy do when he doesn't like dogs but one dog very obviously likes him? Easy-to-read text and irresistible pictures portray this delightful courtship.
32 illustrations in 2 colors; 2-color jacket; 3¾ x 5⅞; 32 pp.
Ages 4-8; grades K-3. *August.* $1.95 $2.19*

HAROLD'S ABC
By CROCKETT JOHNSON, *pictures by the author.* In this seventh book about Harold and his purple crayon, our hero embarks on an ingenious trip through the alphabet.
64 illustrations in 2 colors; 2-color jacket; 4⅝ x 5⅝; 64 pp.
Ages 4-8; grades K-3. *August.* $1.95 $2.19*

3 new I CAN READ Books
Each contains 64 illustrations in 3 colors; full-color jackets; 5⅞ x 8½; 64 pp. Ages 4-8; grades K-3. *October.* $1.95 $2.19*

THE CASE OF THE HUNGRY STRANGER
By CROSBY BONSALL, *pictures by the author.* Somebody had taken the missing blueberry pie. The only question was, who? In this first Mystery I CAN READ Book, by the creator of WHO'S A PEST?, all the club members set out to find the culprit.

GRIZZWOLD
By SYD HOFF, *pictures by the author.* Grizzwold, an enormous bear, is forced to leave his home in the forest. His delectable adventures finding a new (and superior) home will provide untold laughs.

SOLDIERS AND SAILORS /What Do They Do?/
By CARLA GREENE, *pictures by* LEONARD KESSLER. Through the adventures of Soldier Tom and Sailor Jack, young readers will learn about our armed forces and how they are trained to protect our country.

A HOLIDAY FOR MISTER MUSTER
By ARNOLD LOBEL, *pictures by the author.* The characters from A ZOO FOR MISTER MUSTER are back in another happy adventure. This time, Mister Muster takes his animal friends to the seashore — with riotous results.
31 illustrations in 2 colors; 2-color jacket; 10 x 7¼; 32 pp.
Ages 4-8; grades K-3. *September.* $2.75 $2.73*

THE LITTLE GIANT GIRL AND THE ELF BOY
By ELSE HOLMELUND MINARIK, *pictures by* GARTH WILLIAMS. This beautiful, full-color picture book about Little Giant Girl and the very tiny Elf Boy conveys with gentle humor a world large in love and close to the small child's needs. The text is by the author of the famous LITTLE BEAR books.
Illustrations in full color; full-color jacket; 6¼ x 8½; 32 pp.
Ages 4-8; grades K-3. *October.* $2.75 $2.73*

THE MOON IN MY ROOM
By URI SHULEVITZ, *pictures by the author.* A gentle bedtime story, beautifully illustrated, about a little boy and his friend, Prince Bear, with whom he shares the grand kingdom of his room.
32 illustrations in 3 colors; 4-color jacket; 7 x 8¾; 32 pp.
Ages 4-8; grades K-3. *September.* $2.50 $2.67*

SARAH'S ROOM
By DORIS ORGEL, *pictures by* MAURICE SENDAK. Like Sarah, what little girl has not longed to play in an older sister's room? Blithe verse and beguiling pictures tell how Sarah proves worthy of her ambition.
42 illustrations in 3 colors; 3-color jacket; 3¾ x 5¾; 48 pp.
Ages 4-8; grades K-3. *August.* $1.95 $2.19*

THE QUARRELING BOOK
By CHARLOTTE ZOLOTOW, *pictures by* ARNOLD LOBEL. How a little bad temper (on a rainy day!) can go a long way—until a bit of good nature turns the tables. Delightful humor.
31 black and white illustrations; 3-color jacket; 5½ x 6; 32 pp.
Ages 4-8; grades K-3. *August.* $1.95 $2.19*

*Net prices for HARPERCREST bindings available to schools and libraries.
HARPER & ROW, Publishers, 49 East 33rd St., New York 16, N. Y.

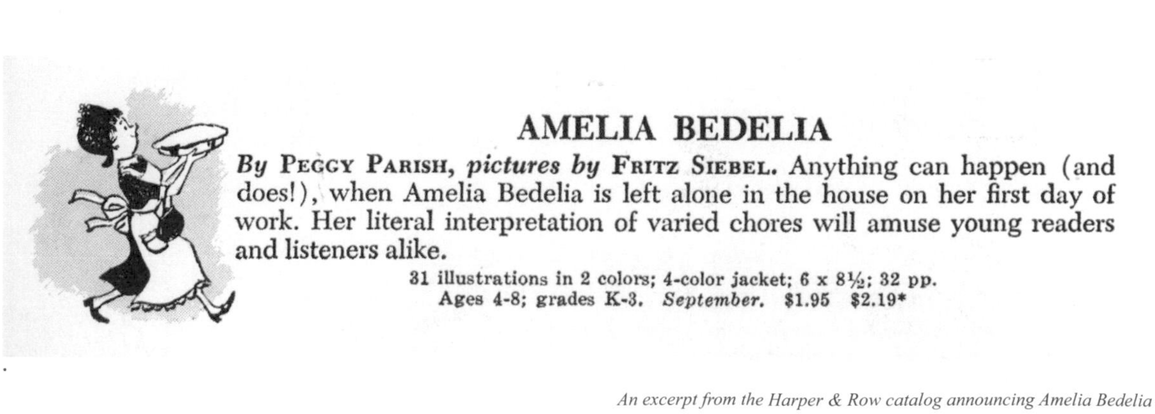

AMELIA BEDELIA
By PEGGY PARISH, *pictures by* FRITZ SIEBEL. Anything can happen (and does!), when Amelia Bedelia is left alone in the house on her first day of work. Her literal interpretation of varied chores will amuse young readers and listeners alike.
31 illustrations in 2 colors; 4-color jacket; 6 x 8½; 32 pp.
Ages 4-8; grades K-3. *September.* $1.95 $2.19*

An excerpt from the Harper & Row catalog announcing Amelia Bedelia

Amelia Bedelia

The Story Behind the Story

Amelia Bedelia, written by Peggy Parish and illustrated by Fritz Siebel, was published in September 1963 by Harper & Row. It was published as a jacketed hardcover picture book, in green and black ink, in a slightly smaller trim size (6 x 8 ½) than the book you are now holding in your hands. *Amelia Bedelia* was edited by Susan Hirschman.

Peggy Parish was born in Manning, South Carolina, on July 14, 1927. She graduated from the University of South Carolina with a degree in English and taught in Oklahoma and Kentucky before spending fifteen years as a teacher at the progressive Dalton School in New York City. In 1961, during her time at Dalton, she published her first book—*Littlest Raccoon*, illustrated by Claude Humbert (Golden Books)—which was followed in 1962 by *Let's Be Indians*, illustrated by Arnold Lobel (Harper & Row) and *My Little Golden Book of Manners*, illustrated by Richard Scarry (Golden Books).

Amelia Bedelia was inspired by the students in her third-grade classroom and their sometimes hilarious mix-ups with vocabulary. Peggy Parish shared classroom anecdotes with her editor, Susan Hirschman, over lunch and tea, and in time the beloved character—who takes every word literally and who embraces life with a straightforward and positive attitude no matter what the circumstances—was born.

"I guess I love mischief as much as Amelia Bedelia. I simply enjoy laughing at life."—Peggy Parish

Peggy Parish wrote twelve books about Amelia Bedelia and published close to fifty books for children, in all. She died on November 18, 1988, in Manning, South Carolina. A statue of Amelia Bedelia, commemorating Peggy Parish's life and the beloved character, was installed in front of the library in her hometown of Manning in 1999. The Amelia Bedelia books are now written by her nephew, Herman Parish, and illustrated by Lynn Sweat and Lynne Avril.

"Children's rights are taken away from them when they enter school. What I try to show teachers is that all the skills needed to read can be taught outside of textbooks. Today's children are not going to read what they are not interested in. And if a positive attitude toward reading is not developed during the first three years of school, it is virtually impossible to develop it later."—Peggy Parish

Frederick (Fritz) Siebel

was born on December 19, 1913, in Vienna, Austria. He attended the School of Applied Arts in Vienna, where he studied illustration and stage design. Fritz Siebel immigrated to the United States in 1936 and worked for Paramount Pictures, designing and illustrating movie posters. In 1938 he entered a competition, judged by Eleanor Roosevelt and others, to create an image to alert Americans to the importance of protecting the nation's security in wartime. His poster, the now iconic "Someone Talked," won numerous awards.

The illustrator, 1962

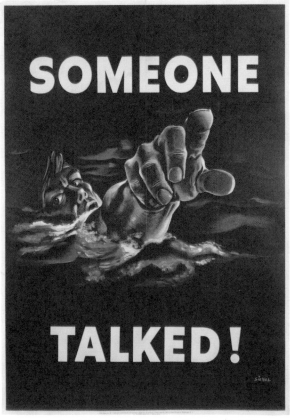

Frederick Siebel's iconic poster was first printed in 1938.

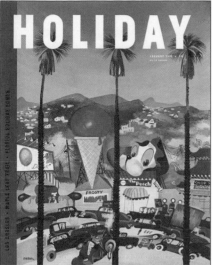

A cover illustration for Holiday *and tear sheets of a Jell-O nursery rhyme ad (Young and Rubicam, 1955–57) and a Textron ad from* The Saturday Evening Post *(1949).*

Fritz Siebel contributed hundreds of editorial illustrations to *Collier's, Holiday,* and *The Saturday Evening Post* and also worked on numerous advertising campaigns, including, starting in 1957, the creation of the well-known Mr. Clean character for the Tatum-Laird advertising agency. In 1960, he founded a graphic and package design company, Frederick Siebel Associates. He applied his talents to package design for products ranging from Captain Morgan Rum to Canada Dry Ginger Ale.

His nursery rhyme–inspired illustrations for a Jell-O campaign brought him to the attention of the children's book department at Random House, and in 1958, Fritz illustrated his first work for children, *A Fly Went By* (Beginner Books, Random House). Shortly thereafter he began illustrating books for Harper & Row, as well. Fritz Siebel illustrated the first three Amelia Bedelia books, and he illustrated twelve children's books in all from 1958–1968, before the strenuous and time-consuming task of creating pre-separated art drove him back to advertising full-time. The artist died in December 1991. His daughter, Barbara Siebel Thomas, worked on the new full-color, expanded I Can Read edition of *Amelia Bedelia*, colorizing her father's illustrations and creating new images for the additional pages.

Fritz Siebel, Peggy Parish, and Susan Hirschman worked together to determine the look for *Amelia Bedelia*. This rough sketch is one of the first character sketches that Fritz Siebel did and was discovered in his papers by his widow, Gretchen Siebel, who remembers Peggy and Susan talking and Fritz drawing as he listened to them.

Character study of Amelia Bedelia, 1962

The original art for *Amelia Bedelia* was pre-separated, which meant that instead of delivering *one* painting for each illustration to the publisher, the artist had to create the image in several layers, with a layer representing each shift in color. Fritz Siebel's dummy book, on the other hand, was painted (in watercolor, ink, and markers) in green and black and includes the original manuscript taped in place, as well as handwritten editorial notes regarding both the text and pictures (shown here).

All of this work was worth it. After fifty years of keeping house, Amelia Bedelia is still delighting new generations of readers.

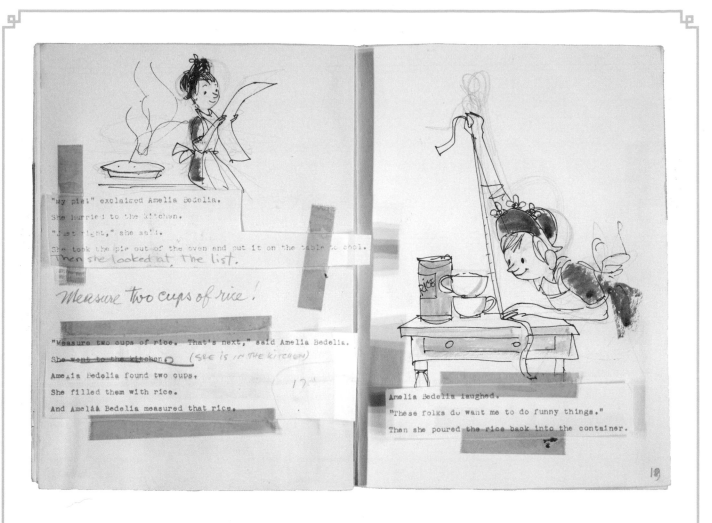

"My pie!" exclaimed Amelia Bedelia.
She hurried to the kitchen.
"Just right," she said.
She took the pie out of the oven and put it on the table to cool.
Then she looked at the list.

Measure two cups of rice!

"Measure two cups of rice. That's next," said Amelia Bedelia.
She went to the kitchen. (SHE IS IN THE KITCHEN)
Amelia Bedelia found two cups.
She filled them with rice.
And Amelia Bedelia measured that rice.

17"

Amelia Bedelia laughed.
"These folks do want me to do funny things."
Then she poured the rice back into the container.

18

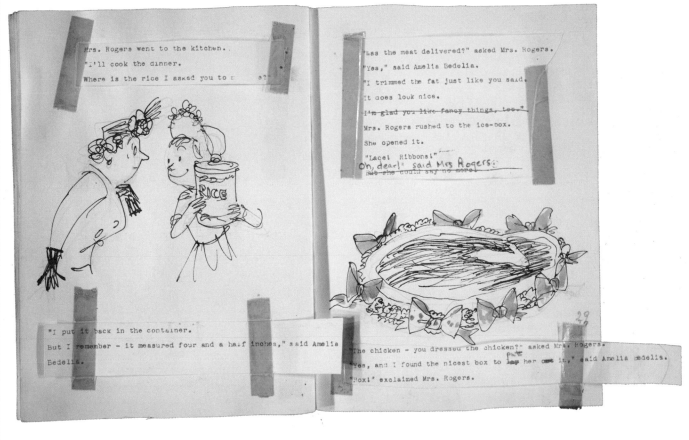

Mrs. Rogers went to the kitchen.
"I'll cook the dinner.
Where is the rice I asked you to m   e?"

"I put it back in the container.
But I remember - it measured four and a half inches," said Amelia
Bedelia.

"Was the meat delivered?" asked Mrs. Rogers.
"Yes," said Amelia Bedelia.
"I trimmed the fat just like you said.
It does look nice.
I'm glad you like fancy things, too."
Mrs. Rogers rushed to the ice-box.
She opened it.
"Lace! Ribbons!
Oh, dear!" said Mrs Rogers.
But she could say no more!

"The chicken - you dressed the chicken?" asked Mrs. Rogers.
"Yes, and I found the nicest box to put her in," said Amelia Bedelia.
"Box!" exclaimed Mrs. Rogers.

29

Changing with the times—
fifty years of Amelia Bedelia